To Summer Rose, Michelle Malia,
and the memory of Uncle Harry K. Mitchell

— D. R.

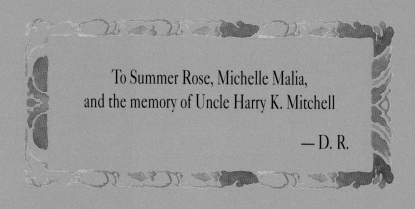

TŪTŪ NĒNĒ
THE HAWAIIAN
MOTHER GOOSE
RHYMES

Written by Debra Ryll
Illustrated by Alexis America

Published and distributed by

ISLAND HERITAGE
PUBLISHING
A DIVISION OF THE MADDEN CORPORATION
99-880 IWAENA STREET, AIEA, HAWAII 96701-3202
PHONE: (808) 487-7299 • FAX: (808) 488-2279
E-MAIL: HAWAII4U@PIXI.COM

ISBN #0-89610-300-5
First Edition, First Printing — 1997

TŪTŪ NĒNĒ
THE HAWAIIAN MOTHER GOOSE
RHYMES

Written by Debra Ryll
Illustrated by Alexis America

ISLAND HERITAGE
P U B L I S H I N G

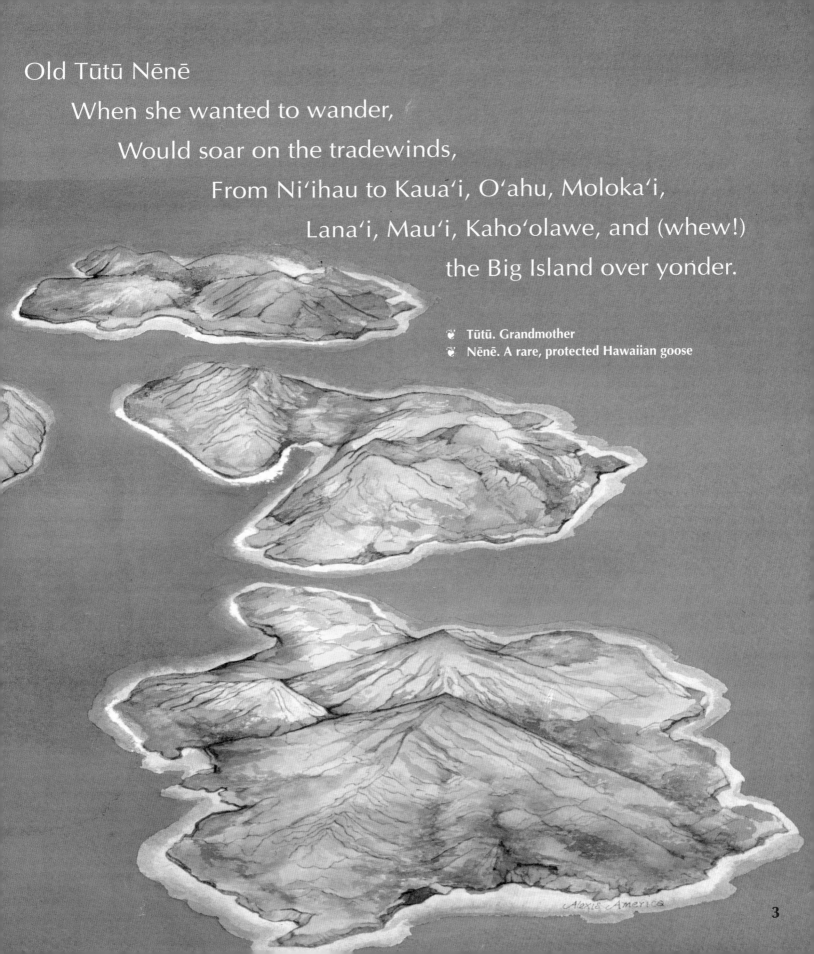

Old Tūtū Nēnē
   When she wanted to wander,
      Would soar on the tradewinds,
         From Niʻihau to Kauaʻi, Oʻahu, Molokaʻi,
            Lanaʻi, Mauʻi, Kahoʻolawe, and (whew!)
              the Big Island over yonder.

   🌺 **Tūtū. Grandmother**
   🌺 **Nēnē. A rare, protected Hawaiian goose**

Little Miss Aku sat on a pōhaku,

Swatting mosquitoes all day.

Along came a spider,

Who sat down beside her

And scared the buggahs away.

Pōhaku. Rock
Buggah. Pidgin English for bug

This little menehune went to the lū'au,
This little menehune stayed home.
This little menehune ate kālua pig,
This little menehune had none.

And this little menehune cried, "Auwē! Auwē!"
All the way home.

🌺 Menehune. Hawaiian elf
🌺 Kālua pig. Pork baked in an imu

🌺 Lū'au. Hawaiian feast
🌺 Auwē! Oh dear! Alas!

6

Find a pig and roast him,

Wrap him in tī.

Bake him in the imu,

For the cousins and me!

🌱 Tī. A woody green plant
🌱 Imu. Underground oven

Sticky rice hot,
Sticky rice cold.
Sour poi in the pot,
Nine days old!

Some like it hot,
Some like it cold.
Some like it in the pot,
Nine days old!

🍠 Poi. Pounded taro

Fish-cake! Fish-cake!

Rice and Spam.

Make me a plate lunch,

As fast as you can!

🐝 Fish-cake. Pressed seafood, used in local dishes
🐝 Spam. A favorite Island food
🐝 Plate lunch. Hawaiian "fast food"

Sumo Takahashi sat on the wall,
Sumo Takahashi had a great fall.
And all King Kalākaua's horses, and all of his men,
Couldn't put Mr. Takahashi up on that wall again.

🐢 Sumo. A very large wrestler
🐢 Kalākaua. A famous Hawaiian king

10

The itsy bitsy bufo
Went up the cane shack spout.
Down came the rain
And washed the bufo out.
Up came the lā
And dried up all the rain.
And the itsy bitsy bufo
Went up the spout again.

🐸 **Bufo**. Toad   🐸 **Lā**. Sun   11

Pi'ilani picked a peck of pickled poke.

A peck of pickled poke Pi'ilani picked.

If Pi'ilani picked a peck of pickled poke,

Where's the peck of pickled poke Pi'ilani picked?

(Polihale, probably.)

🐚 Poke. Sliced fish, eaten raw
🐚 Polihale. A beach on the island of Kaua'i.

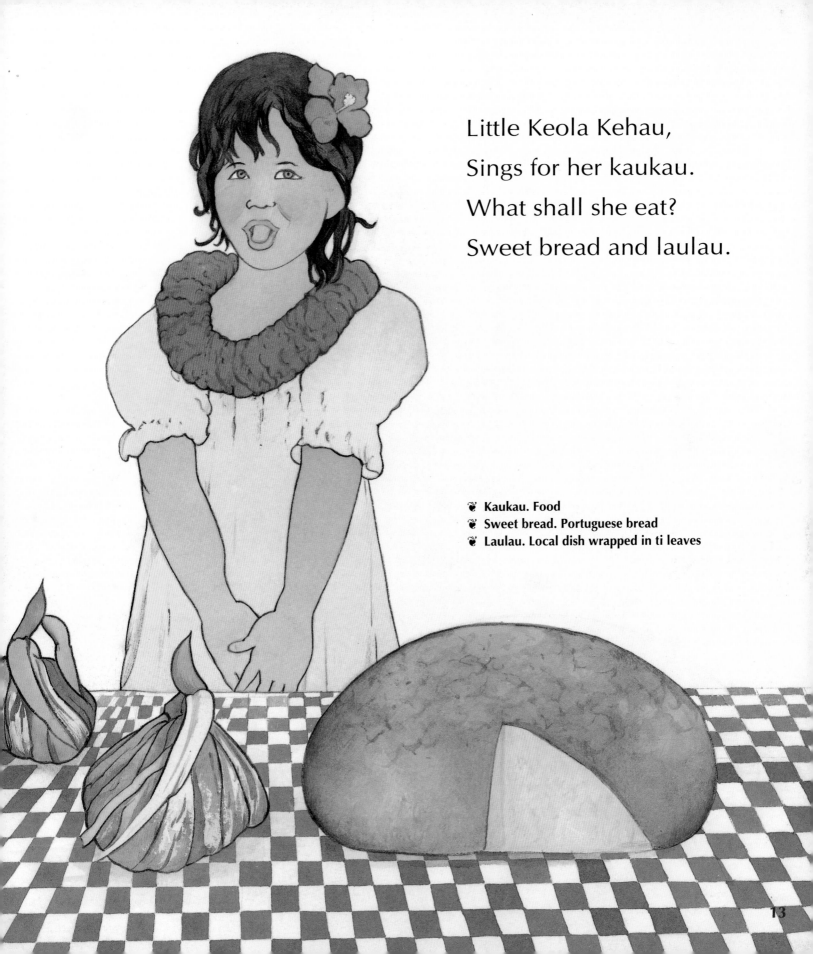

Little Keola Kehau,
Sings for her kaukau.
What shall she eat?
Sweet bread and laulau.

🌺 **Kaukau.** Food
🌺 **Sweet bread.** Portuguese bread
🌺 **Laulau.** Local dish wrapped in ti leaves

Little Kekoa sat in a corner,

Eating his liliko'i pie.

He put in his thumb,

Took out a crumb,

And said,

    "'Ono ka mea'ai!"

🌺 Liliko'i. Passion fruit
🌺 'Ono. Delicious
14 🌺 Mea'ai. Food

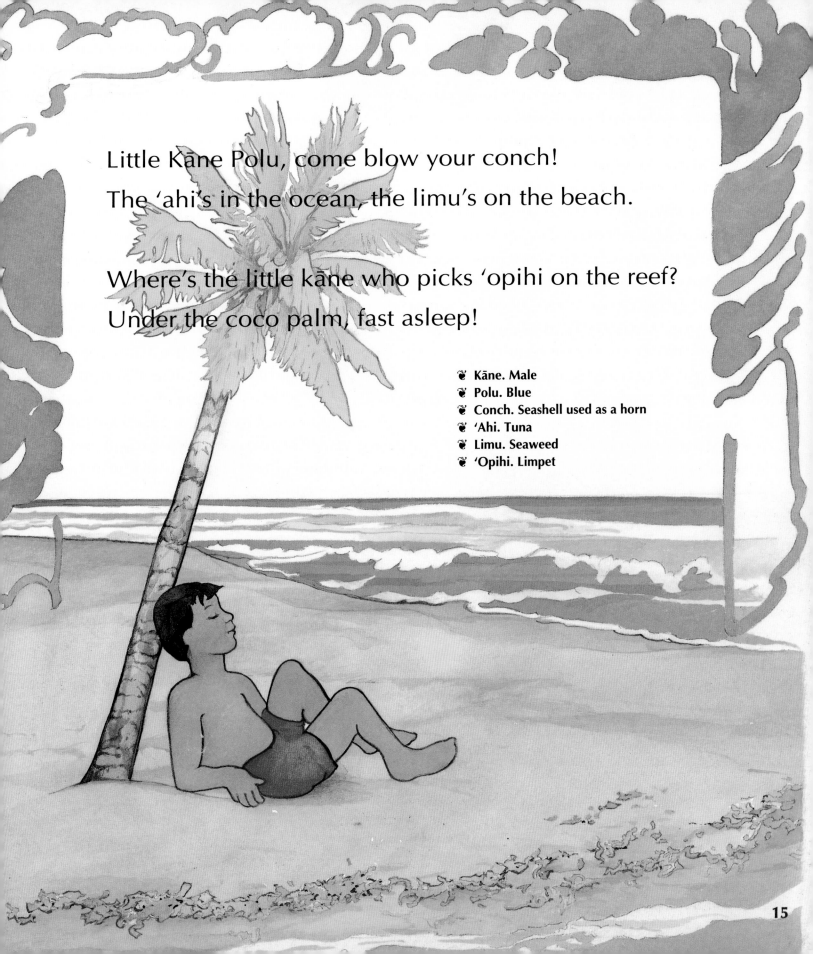

Little Kāne Polu, come blow your conch!

The 'ahi's in the ocean, the limu's on the beach.

Where's the little kāne who picks 'opihi on the reef?

Under the coco palm, fast asleep!

🐚 **Kāne.** Male
🐚 **Polu.** Blue
🐚 **Conch.** Seashell used as a horn
🐚 **'Ahi.** Tuna
🐚 **Limu.** Seaweed
🐚 **'Opihi.** Limpet

Old Tūtū Pele sang a fierce mele,

And the lava flowed into the sea.

When it got there,

Kalapana was bare,

So Pele made sand for a beach.

🐚 **Tūtū. Grandmother**
🐚 **Pele. Volcano Goddess**
🐚 **Mele. Song or chant**
🐚 **Lava. Volcanic rock**
🐚 **Kalapana. A black sand beach on the Big Island**

Malia had a little mo'o,

Its skin was green and yellow.

And everywhere Malia went,

The mo'o was sure to holoholo.

It followed her to school one day,

Which was against the kumu's rule.

It made the keiki laugh and play,

To see a mo'o at school.

- 🌺 Mo'o. Gecko or lizard
- 🌺 Holoholo. Go
- 🌺 Kumu. Teacher
- 🌺 Keiki. Child

Kaleo Kalani,

Haupia and pie,

Kissed the wahine and made them cry.

When the kāne came out to play,

Kaleo Kalani ran away.

🌺 **Haupia.** Coconut pudding
🌺 **Wahine.** Women
🌺 **Kāne.** Male

Ring around the pua nani,

Pocket full of loke lani.

Lehu, lehu!

We all fall down.

🐚 **Pua.** Flower
🐚 **Loke lani.** Small red rose

🐚 **Nani.** Beautiful
🐚 **Lehu.** Ashes

Little Hoʻkipa has a puka in her net,

And doesn't know how to mend it.

Leave her alone, when the ʻohana comes home,

With kōkua they'll surely tend it.

🐚 **Puka.** Hole
🐚 **ʻOhana.** Family
🐚 **Kōkua.** Help, assistance

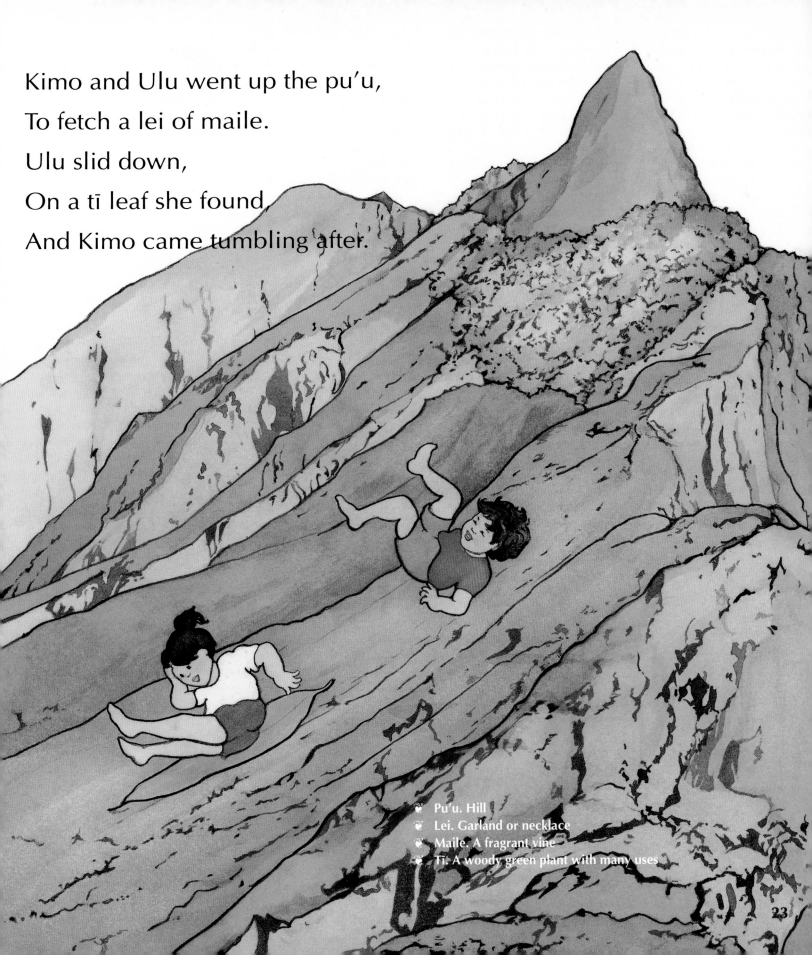

Kimo and Ulu went up the puʻu,

To fetch a lei of maile.

Ulu slid down,

On a tī leaf she found,

And Kimo came tumbling after.

Puʻu. Hill
Lei. Garland or necklace
Maile. A fragrant vine
Tī. A woody green plant with many uses

23

Twinkle, twinkle little hōkū,

How I wonder all about you.

Up above the 'āina so high,

Like a kaimana in the sky.

🌺 Hōkū. Star
🌺 'Āina. Land, earth
🌺 Kaimana. Diamond

Deedle, deedle wonton, my boy Quan,

Went to bed with his tabis on.

One slippah off, one slippah on,

Deedle, deedle wonton, my boy Quan.

🍎 **Wonton.** A Chinese appetizer
🍎 **Tabis.** Sock-like slippers
🍎 **Slippah.** Pidgin English for slipper

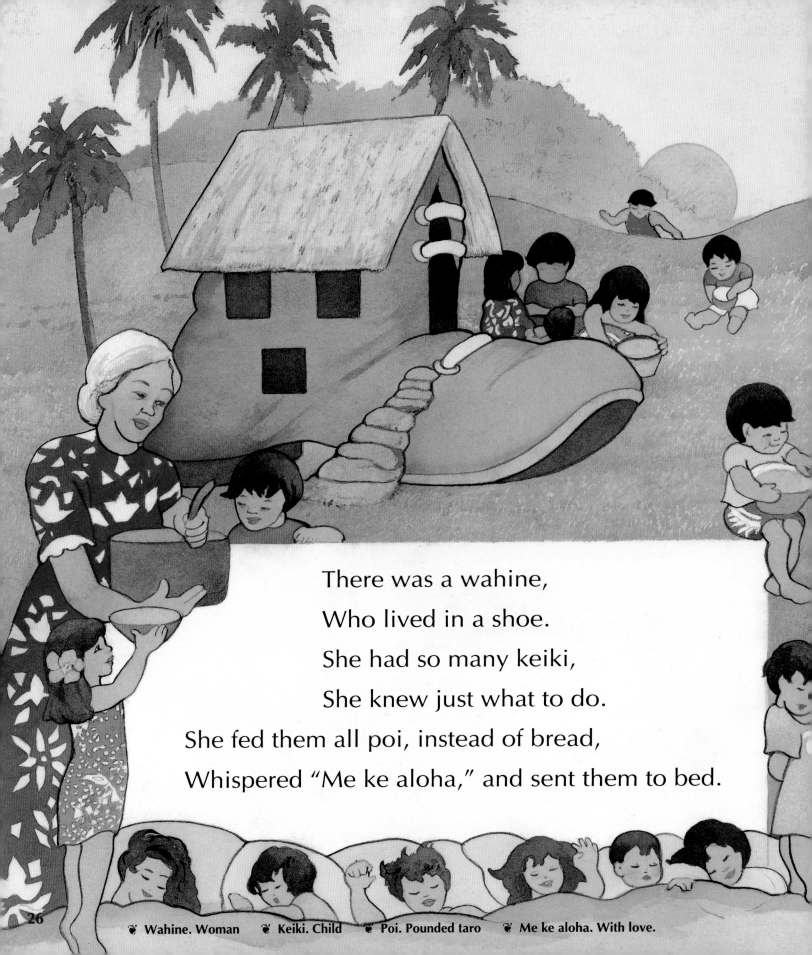

There was a wahine,

Who lived in a shoe.

She had so many keiki,

She knew just what to do.

She fed them all poi, instead of bread,

Whispered "Me ke aloha," and sent them to bed.

26

🌺 **Wahine.** Woman   🌺 **Keiki.** Child   🌺 **Poi.** Pounded taro   🌺 **Me ke aloha.** With love.

Ua, ua, go away,

Hilo's wet enough today,

And all the tourists want to play!

🐚 **Ua. Rain**

🐚 **Hilo. A rainy town on the Big Island**

Here is the 'ohana,
Here are the kūpuna.
Open your heart,
And feel the aloha.

28   🐾 'Ohana. Family   🐾 Kūpuna. Ancestor   🐾 Aloha. Love